WOODLAND TALES

Pipkin The Shy Pixie

"My sauccpan's fallen to pieces," wailed Pixie Pipkin, as his breakfast porridge spilt all over the cooking stove.

"Ho, ho," he heard a voice chuckling from the hollow tree where he lived. "What are you going to do now, Pipkin?"

Pipkin stepped outside his front door and looked up at Old Oaky, who was grinning from branch to branch. "It's all very well for you to laugh," cried Pipkin, stamping his foot. "You *know* I can't buy a new saucepan."

"And why not?" asked Oaky, raising one thick, bark eyebrow.

"Because . . . because . . ." mumbled Pipkin, then he stopped, went very red and hung his head.

"Because you're too shy," said Oaky. Pipkin nodded and looked miserable.

Oaky rustled his leaves in a big sigh and said, more kindly, "I wish I could think of a cure for you, Pipkin. But if you're too shy to go and buy a new saucepan, you'll have to look for a second-hand one."

"Where can I find a second-hand saucepan?" asked Pipkin.

"Just beyond the woodlands is a dump where the woodland gnomes put all the rubbish that silly people dump in our forest. That's where you may find an old saucepan."

Oaky pointed the way with one of his branches and Pipkin hurried away between the long grass and ferns. Suddenly a big black cat leapt across his path and Pipkin nearly jumped out of his skin.

"Oh, Tiptoes, you *did* give me a fright," he gasped. Tiptoes looked at him curiously. "What are you doing out so early, Pipkin?" she purred.

"I'm going to the rubbish dump to look for a saucepan," said Pipkin.

Tiptoes followed him to the edge of the wood. Beyond the trees lay the rubbish dump and Pipkin looked at it in amazement. There were old bedsteads, worn-out car tyres, cracked cups and broken flowerpots.

"I can't see anything small enough to use as a saucepan," frowned Pipkin, as he started searching round the rubbish dump. But at last he found an empty tin can. "If I fix a handle to this, it will do very well," he decided.

As he looked for a piece of metal to make a handle, he suddenly saw something moving in front of him. IT WAS ANOTHER PIXIE.

Pipkin felt so shy he dropped the can and ran off as fast as his legs would carry him. He dived behind one of the broken flowerpots and hid there, his heart going thumpity-thump.

When at last he got his breath back, Pipkin peeped out again. A little way off was another flowerpot and peeping round it was the other pixie.

Pipkin bobbed out of sight again. Then he thought: "That other pixie must be as shy as I am."

So he peeped out from his flowerpot and waved. The other pixie waved at Pipkin at just the same time. "He must want to be friends," thought Pipkin.

Pipkin came out from behind his flowerpot and so did the other pixie. Pipkin drew a deep breath and was about to call to the other pixie, when he heard a loud noise.

It was some gnomes and their lorry arriving with a load of rubbish. Both pixies ran back to their flowerpots. Pipkin hid behind his, trembling, as the lorry came closer and closer. Then a voice called: "Tip it up here, Bill!"

Pipkin looked out just in time to see a whole load of rubbish falling over the place where the other pixie was hiding. "What shall I do?" he cried, as the lorry drove away. "I'll never be able to dig through all that rubbish and rescue the other pixie. I must get help!"

Pipkin rushed away from the dump and dashed along a woodland path, wondering where he could find help. Then he saw the Wise Witch's cottage.

Quite forgetting that he'd never, ever spoken to the Wise Witch before, he banged on her door.

"Who's knocking on my door?" demanded the Wise Witch.

"Please come and help," cried Pipkin, running inside. "My pixie friend's had a load of rubbish tipped over him and I can't move it myself." And he burst into tears.

Just then there came a loud 'meow' and Tiptoes jumped in through the window and onto the witch's shoulder, purring something into her ear.

"Close your eyes, Pipkin," said the witch. "You musn't look while I make some special magic."

"Oh, do hurry," sobbed Pipkin, as he shut his eyes. He kept them tightly closed while the witch moved around the room, chanting some strange words.

"Now you can open your eyes again," said the witch.

Pipkin opened his eyes and there, standing in front of him, was the other pixie. He looked as though *he'd* been crying, too. But then both pixies clapped their hands and ran towards each other.

Suddenly, Pipkin's head hit something hard and he fell back, onto the floor. "Ooh," he cried. "That other pixie *hit* me."

"There was no other pixie," laughed the witch. "You were looking at your own reflection in an old piece of looking glass on the rubbish dump. You didn't know who it was because you've always been too shy to buy a mirror."

Pipkin burst into tears again. "Then I haven't got a friend after all," he sobbed. "You were just teasing me," he cried.

Before the Wise Witch could stop him, he rushed out of her cottage and ran back along the woodland path. He was in such a temper, he didn't see someone else coming towards him in a hurry.

BUMP! Once again Pipkin banged his head against something hard. "Oh," he cried, as he saw another pixie rubbing his own head. "That witch is playing tricks on me again."

"Why did you hit me?" shouted the other pixie, angrily, coming towards Pipkin with his fists up.

They were just going to start fighting when Pipkin thought of something. "Why, you're real," he cried.

"What are you talking about?" asked Popper, the other pixie.

"I thought . . . ho, ho . . . I thought . . . hee, hee, that you were my reflection," giggled Pipkin.

He explained how the witch had tricked him and then Popper started laughing. They giggled so much that tears ran down their faces.

"Wait till the others hear about this," laughed Popper, leading Pipkin into a big glade. In the middle of the glade grew the tall ash tree where Popper lived with Hopper and Topper.

Asleep

Popper told them all about the trick the witch had played on Pipkin and they thought it was very funny. "You were brave, going to see the Wise Witch all by yourself," said Topper.

"What were you doing at the rubbish dump in the first place?" asked Hopper.

"I went to look for a second-hand saucepan," said Pipkin, suddenly remembering that he still hadn't one.

"Why not get a new saucepan from the Woodland Stores?" asked Popper. "Come along, we'll go with you and buy you one as a present."

So off they went, arm in arm, until they came to Big Beechy, the largest tree in the woodlands. Hanging from one branch was a notice with WOODLAND STORES painted on it.

The other pixies led Pipkin through the main entrance, between two big tree roots. "We'll take a shopping trolley, just for fun," said Hopper.

As soon as they got inside the stores they found the whole place was crowded with other pixies doing their early morning shopping. Pipkin had never seen so many pixies before. He didn't know so many lived in the woodlands. To his surprise he found it all very exciting.

Hopper and Topper pushed the trolley with Pipkin and Popper riding on top. They went all round the shop until they came to the shelves of pots and pans.

"What size saucepan do you need?" asked Hopper, picking up a huge one.

"I only need a small one for my breakfast porridge," said Pipkin. He suddenly remembered he hadn't had any breakfast yet and was feeling very hungry.

"Let's buy a big one as well, for when you have visitors," said Hopper.

So they chose a big saucepan and a small one, and then went to the cash desk to pay for them. "Now we'll help you carry them home," said Popper.

Old Oaky's bark mouth dropped open when he saw them coming. "What ever has happened to Pipkin the shy pixie?" he asked.

"He's made some friends at last," said Tiptoes, who was waiting on the doorstep. "The Wise Witch will be pleased!"

She meowed as Pipkin started to open the door. "The Wise Witch is sorry you were so upset by her little joke, so she sent me along with some *real* magic to make up for it."

Tiptoes dropped a small bag of herbs into the big saucepan and said: "Now put it on the stove to boil and see what happens."

So Pipkin started making porridge with the witch's magic herbs. "That smells so good it's making us all feel hungry," said Popper.

At last the porridge was ready and Pipkin poured some into acorn cups for everyone. Then he gave Tiptoes a large saucer of milk.

Popper, Hopper, Topper and Pipkin sat outside, under Oaky's branches, and began their breakfast. The porridge tasted better than anything they had ever eaten before.

"We'll come and have breakfast with you again," said Hopper, as he started his third helping.

"It was very lucky you bumped into Popper," said Topper. "Now we shall be able to have lots of fun together."